Anthony Browne

WILLY THE WIZARD

Red Fox

A Red Fox Book

Published by Random House Children's Books
20 Vauxhall Bridge Road, London SW1V 2SA

A division of Random House UK Ltd
London Melbourne Sydney Auckland
Johannesburg and agencies throughout the world

3 5 7 9 10 8 6 4

First published by Julia MacRae 1995
Red Fox edition 1996

Printed in Singapore by
Tien Wah Press (Pte) Ltd

RANDOM HOUSE UK Limited Reg. No. 954009

ISBN 0 09 953761 3

For Nicholas, Francesca and Jacqueline

Willy loved football. But there was a problem –
he didn't have any boots. He couldn't afford them.

Willy went eagerly to the practice sessions
every week. He ran and chased and harried,
but no-one passed the ball to him.
He was never picked for the team.

One evening, when Willy was walking home past the
old pie factory, he saw someone kicking a ball around.
The stranger was wearing old-fashioned soccer gear, like
the clothes Willy remembered his dad wearing.
But he was good. Very good.

Willy watched for a while and when the ball came
over to him he kicked it back. They played
silently together, passing the ball to and fro.

Then the stranger did something very odd.
He unlaced his boots, took them off, and without
saying a word he handed them to Willy.

Willy stared at them with wonder.

When he looked up,
no-one was there.

Taking great care not to step
on any cracks in the pavement,
Willy carried the boots home.

He cleaned and polished
them until they looked new.

Then he went slowly upstairs,
counting *every* step (sixteen),
washed his hands and face *very* thoroughly,
brushed his teeth for *exactly* four minutes,
put on his pyjamas (always the top first,
always with *four* buttons fastened),
used the lavatory, and dived into bed.
(He had to be in bed before the
flushing stopped, for who knows what would
happen if he wasn't?)
Every morning he repeated all these
actions in reverse. *Every* morning.

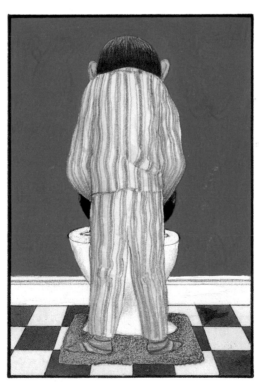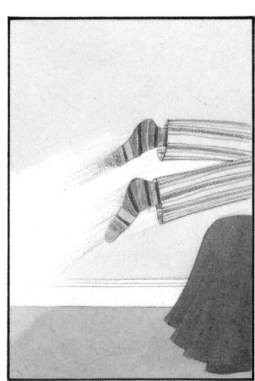

For the next football practice Willy proudly
took along his boots. But the other players
weren't exactly impressed . . .

. . . until they saw him play.

Wearing the old boots, Willy was fantastic!

When the captain pinned up the
team for next Saturday's match,
Willy could hardly believe his eyes.

He was so pleased that he ran all the way home
(being very careful not to step on the cracks).

Every day Willy wore his boots and practised
shooting, dribbling, passing and heading.
He got better and better. Willy was sure
his boots were magic.

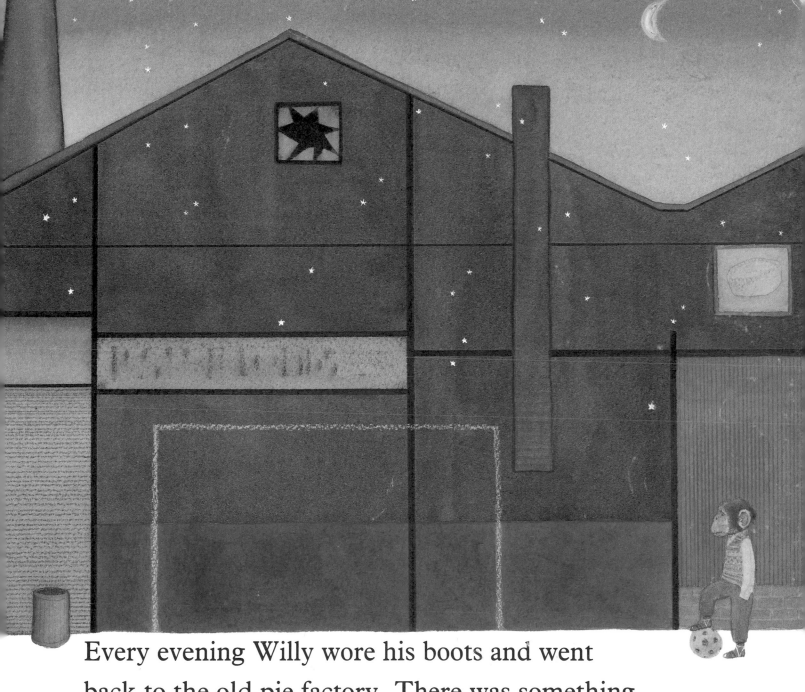

Every evening Willy wore his boots and went
back to the old pie factory. There was something
curiously familiar about the stranger which made
Willy want to see him again. But he was never there.

On Friday night Willy went through his
usual bedtime routine.

He went slowly upstairs counting *every* step
(still sixteen),

washed his hands and face *very* thoroughly,

brushed his teeth for *exactly* four minutes,

put on his pyjamas (the top first, with
four buttons fastened),

used the lavatory, and dived into bed
before the flushing stopped (phew!).

But Willy was too excited to sleep.
Even when he drifted off, he spent an
uncomfortable night dreaming of disasters.

In the morning, he woke up with a start.
It was 9.45 and the match started at 10!
He leaped out of bed,
threw on his clothes,
raced down the stairs
and dashed out of the door.

Willy ran all the way to the football ground.

When he got there the other players were already
changed. The captain threw Willy his kit and he
put it on. Then the awful thought struck him . . .
HE HAD FORGOTTEN HIS BOOTS!
Someone found him another pair.
"Y-you don't understand . . ." he said, but the
team had already gone onto the pitch.

The crowd's roar turned to laughter when Willy
emerged from the dressing-room. Willy grinned,
but inside he felt angry.

The game started. Willy was amazed how fast it
was. Within minutes the opposition had scored.
One—nil! From the restart the ball shot out to
Willy on the wing. He hadn't time to think, he
just ran with the ball at his feet.

Willy was magic – the ball seemed to be attached to him by an invisible thread. He dribbled past three opponents and sent in a perfect cross. GOAL!

It seemed that Willy could do no wrong.
Every time he got the ball the opposition was
mesmerised. The teams were very evenly
matched. With seconds to go the score was still
1—1. The ball was passed to Willy in defence. He
beat one player, then another, and another, and
another, until he'd got past the whole team.

Only the goalkeeper to beat. The keeper
was huge and the net looked tiny.
Could Willy do it?

He could! The crowd was spellbound as Willy conjured up the perfect shot. GOALLLLL ! ! !

"WILLY THE WIZARD! WILLY THE WIZARD!"
chanted the crowd.

Later, on the way home,
Willy thought about the
boots and the stranger.
And he smiled.